The Ghost of Grannoch Moor

The Ghost of

Grannoch Moor

William MacKellar

ILLUSTRATED BY TED LEWIN

DODD, MEAD & COMPANY
New York

Weekly Reader Children's Book Club Edition

For the students of
John J. Jennings School
Bristol, Connecticut

The Ghost of Grannoch Moor

Chapter 1

Davie Cameron frowned. "Colonel Blaikie has a new dog?" He turned his head and regarded the gentle-faced little man sitting alongside him on the dry-stone dike. "Queer, I have not seen him."

Fergus Gow closed one eye in a solemn wink. Fergus liked to be the bearer of news. The loose yellow skin bunched around the closed eye. "One of those German dogs ye will have heard about, Davie Cameron."

The boy stared. "A German shepherd?"

The little man bobbed his head eagerly. The movement caused the uncombed white hair to spill over his brow. "Aye. Och and a terrible-looking creature it is for certain! All teeth and murderous eyes that glower at ye like two hot coals!" His shoulders shivered under the faded blue shirt. "Now tell me this, Davie Cameron, what for should a man be wanting with a fierce foreign creature like that when he could have a good Scots dog like Bonnie, here?"

The boy nodded and glanced down at the black-and-white Border collie that lay curled up in the heather just below where he sat on the dike. He dangled a bare foot against the fine-spun hair. The dog blinked an eye open but did not stir from where she lay, her body pressed against the coolness of the dike. "That will be true, Fergus. It is strange, as you say, that a man would want one of those fierce foreign dogs in these parts. Aye, and with so many grand Scots dogs for the asking."

"There has to be a reason for that, Davie Cameron! And I will tell ye something, lad. I know what that reason is!" Again Fergus Gow closed his eye in an elaborate wink.

"You do, Fergus?" The boy waited for the little man to continue. Some there were in the village of Wee Clachmannan who thought Fergus Gow a little touched in the head, but Davie did not think so. Just because Fergus had never learned to read or tell the time did not mean that he was simple. Fergus knew other things. More important things.

10

Besides, as Fergus had said on more than one occasion, what was the point of knowing time if you didn't have a watch? Och, and a terrible vanity it would be to have all that wisdom of knowing how the big black hands chased the wee ones around the numbers and no watch at all of one's own! Fergus was like that. Clever where he had to be clever. Like now. Davie leaned forward on the dike. "And why, now, Fergus would Colonel Blaikie be getting himself such a huge dog?"

"It is simple, lad. Ye will be remembering that Colonel Blaikie lives all by himself in that big house of his in the middle of Grannoch Moor. My sister Annie used to say there was a ghost in Rowan House. She said she had even seen it herself when she was a wee lass. Maybe the Colonel has seen it too, since he bought Rowan House. That's why he got himself this big brute of a dog. I've never heard tell that German shepherds were over friendly with ghosts."

Davie smiled but did not answer. He was thinking that Colonel Blaikie of the ramrod straight back, the fierce blue eyes, and the fiercer military mustache could well handle himself in Rowan House if any ghost showed up. Of course, it could simply have been that, living all by himself in the loneliness of Grannoch Moor, Colonel Blaikie had felt the need of some sort of companionship. Strange, though, if that had been the case, he had not gotten himself a decent Scots dog like Bonnie.

Bonnie. Davie looked down at the small collie drowsing at his feet, her body moving gently as she breathed. No, the colonel could scarcely have got a dog like Bonnie. There was only one Bonnie. Had only been one, as long as he could remember. His father, Alec Cameron, had bought Bonnie just two years before he died. Bonnie had gone out with him when he herded his sheep, and there had been no dog more clever with them than the wise little black-and-white collie. With Alec Cameron's death, though, the sheep had been sold and Bonnie had become Davie's responsibility, if you could call her that. There had been no day since then that she had not been a part of, no adventure she had not shared, no grief she had not lightened by just being around. No, Colonel Blaikie could scarcely have found himself a dog quite as fine as Bonnie. Still, he could have done a lot better than he had done, based on what old Fergus Gow had just said.

Davie smiled at the seamed brown face of the little man alongside him. Fergus was chewing on one of the endless squares of grubby yellow cheese he always carried around with him. The faded blue dungarees he wore must have come equipped with cavernous pockets, for Davie had never known Fergus to run short of cheese cubes, no matter how many he popped into his mouth. He never offered Davie any, having opined once that it was a vanity to squander good cheese on boys when there wasn't enough to go around as it was. Fergus held, too, that cheese was good for the brain and maybe if he ate enough he might yet be able to learn to read. As Fergus was at least sixty and had eaten more cheese in his life than all of Wee Clachmannan put together, there were those in the village who winked behind his back and said that maybe Fergus ate too *much* cheese and that his brain had somehow curdled as a result. It wasn't said unkindly, though, or with any malice. There was no one in Wee Clachmannan who did not have an affection for gentle Fergus Gow, despite his sometimes strange behavior. Least of all Davie Cameron.

The boy squinted up at the sun overhead and slid down from the dike. "Have to be getting along, Fergus. I told my mother I'd help her stack the peats. The cow's been off her food, too. Keeps throwing everything up."

Fergus grunted. "Cows are queer that way. What will ye have been feeding her, now?"

Davie shrugged. "Lately we've been giving her turnips with her heather and hay—"

14

"Turnips?" Fergus screwed up his face in an expression of disgust. "Away with ye, Davie Cameron! Turnips are no' fit for human beings, far less cows! Go home now and boil some seaweed and mash it up with salt herring and a wee bit of good Scotch oatmeal. Never met a cow that wasn't daft for a dish like that." He groped in his pocket for another piece of cheese. "And ye can be certain she'll no' be throwing anything up, for nothing sticks to the ribs like oatmeal, herring, and seaweed. Aye, nothing at all."

Davie smiled. "I'll take your word for it, Fergus."

"Sticks to the ribs," Fergus muttered, his vacant eyes fixed in space. "Mind ye tell Kate Cameron that." He did not seem to notice as Davie took his leave, his thoughts apparently elsewhere. "Sticks to the ribs," he said again, then frowned down at the small square of cheese between his fingers as though wondering how it had got there. "Cheese, too," he said, as he popped it into his toothless mouth.

Davie walked swiftly with Bonnie at his heels, not because he was in any particular hurry to get home, but because his legs seemed so light and charged with strength that it would have been an effort to have walked any slower. The keen mountain air fairly sang in his lungs, urging him on. From somewhere near at hand his ears caught the peevish, scolding cry of a lapwing. He breasted a small hill and paused for a moment as the long sweep of Grannoch Moor rose up to meet him. Surely, in all of Scotland, there was no lonelier place than Grannoch Moor. A wasteland of rocks, sparse yellow grass, and huddled clumps of heather, it stretched endlessly into the distance. Only the distant outline of a large, black, stone house broke the flatness of the scene. He frowned as his eyes focused on the grim structure, snarled in a net of vines and ivy like some trapped, dark monster. Odd that Colonel Blaikie had chosen to live in the desolation of Rowan House. Of course, there was always the ghost to keep him company. But then, almost certainly, Colonel Blaikie didn't believe in ghosts. In a way that was too bad, as at least he wouldn't have felt quite so all alone in the huge house. But then maybe he liked it that way.

With Bonnie at his heels, Davie broke into a trot and darted across a small brae. His bare feet rose and fell rhythmically as he made his way across a field of fine, sweet turf freckled with buttercups and wild moor flowers. He swept past the edge of a small peat hag and the moisture oozing from the soft ground was a cold caress against the soles of his feet. Too soon his eyes caught the feathers of smoke from the chimneys of the slate-roofed cottages of Wee Clachmannan. Reluctantly, he slowed his pace, for he did not want his mother to think he had been anxious to get home. Mothers were funny like that. They had this idea that if you were hanging around the house you had nothing to do and before you knew it you were stacking peats to dry out or bringing in wood for the fireplace.

Kate Cameron looked up from her dress she was basting as the kitchen door slowly swung in to admit her son. Her eyes moved to the wag-o'-the-wall clock above the fireplace. "You're late, Davie." She glanced down again at the hem of the dress on her lap. "You'll find some oatcakes and butter on the dresser."

He munched quietly, content to let the rough texture of the oatcakes rest against his tongue. He swallowed slowly to preserve the flavor as long as possible. Nothing on earth tasted half so good as his mother's oatcakes. His tongue pursued the last of the coarse meal crumbs from behind his teeth. "I was talking to Fergus," he said finally. "That's why I was late."

"Fergus?" She shook her head, then let a small smile have its way with her mouth. "Poor old soul. I'm afraid he still grieves for his sister Annie. She brought him up and took care of him since their mother died. Don't know how Fergus gets along without her and him with no schooling at all."

"Aye, but he's a clever one just the same," Davie said loyally. "Nobody in Wee Clachmannan knows the things that Fergus knows. About changlings, and mermaids, and kelpies that can turn into big black horses. He even saw such a horse himself once as it came out of the deep pool in Grannoch Moor. He just missed seeing the kelpie himself."

Kate Cameron's mouth moved as she smoothed the bunched material on which she was working. Perhaps she was smiling to herself. Finally she glanced up and put aside her needle. "Well, enough of all this talk about kelpies and big black horses. We don't have a horse to worry about, but we have a cow, and the same one is sick and not eating at all. What do we do about that, Davie Cameron?"

He grinned triumphantly. "Och, now, and I thought you would never ask me! I mentioned to Fergus she was sick and he told me what we should do."

"Fergus?" she repeated doubtfully.

"Seaweed, oatmeal, and salt herring! You make a mash and give it to her. Fergus says that nothing sticks to the ribs like seaweed, oatmeal, and herring."

His mother's face was a battleground of conflicting emotions. Finally she sighed and, laying aside the dress on which she had been working, took

18

down a biscuit tin from the mantlepiece. "I must be going daft myself to believe the likes of poor Fergus Gow, but it can do no harm. Maggie's not eating anyway." She removed a few coins from the tin and gave them to her son. "Run along to Mr. MacAndrew's shop and get a dozen big herring. And be careful he doesn't slip a few wee ones in when you're not looking."

Davie smiled. "I'll be looking." He turned to the dog. "Come along, Bonnie. No scraps for dogs, though. Not from the fish shop." He stopped suddenly as he swung open the door. "By the way, talking about dogs, Fergus was telling me that Colonel Blaikie has a new one. A German shepherd, no less. Fergus saw it. Now, why would the man want a big fierce creature like that when he could have a collie like Bonnie? Wee Clachmannan raises the best collies in the world, as well he knows."

"Colonel Blaikie will be knowing his own business, Davie, as you should be knowing your own," she said firmly. "Now off with you and keep your eyes open in the fish shop! Mr. MacAndrew charges as much for his wee herring as his big ones, so there's no sense at all in making him rich at our expense."

The boy grinned as he closed the door. "I'm no' a Cameron for nothing! I'll be watching. Come

19

along, Bonnie."

With the little collie at his heels, Davie swung up the gravel path from the cottage and onto the unpaved road that led down to the village. He had only proceeded a few yards along the road when he heard it, a rasping growl, low and menacing from somewhere behind the screen of thick briars to his right. Turning, he caught a glimpse of a massive head of bristly brown hair. He watched, too astonished to speak or move, as a huge shepherd dog slid into view from behind the hedge of briars. Mesmerized, he stared as it crept forward, its ears flat, its body low, its eyes bright with an intense awareness, to where Bonnie stood.

"Bonnie!" He heard the cry break from his lips as he suddenly realized the intent of the big dog. With a bound he lunged forward and felt his fingers tighten around the body of the little collie as it courageously advanced to meet the attack of the newcomer. Davie spun around in the dust of the road so that his body was between the two dogs. There was a low snarl from somewhere just to his left, and he ducked his head as the big shepherd dog tensed to spring.

Chapter 2

"Juno! To me, girl!"

Davie heard the sharp voice from somewhere above and behind where he crouched on the road. Desperately, he held onto the struggling body in his arms. He was hardly surprised that the scrappy little Border collie was in no way intimidated by the larger dog. Davie knew the breed as among the most fearless, which was one of the reasons he had seized the collie as he had. Bonnie would have been just daft enough to have met the other head on. It was in her blood to have done so, as protector of the sheep. And Davie knew that Bonnie was true to her blood.

"Juno!" Again the boy heard the voice crack

like a whip. For a long moment there was silence, then he felt the pressure of strong fingers on his shoulders. "You can get up now, boy."

He blinked his eyes open and stared up at the speaker, a tall man of about middle age dressed in a rumpled, herringbone-tweed suit. A trim military-type mustache, flecked with gray, adorned the man's upper lip, and a broad, hooked nose seemed to act as a peacemaker between two piercing, truculent eyes. His cheeks were red, either from a great deal of sun and rain or a great deal of temper. Davie did not have to be told who the speaker was. Colonel Blaikie.

"Hang it all, boy, will you please get up?" the colonel thundered as though addressing a battalion of his former Black Watch troops. His florid face seemed to be getting even more florid, if that were possible. Finally, with an effort he choked his voice to a lower pitch. "I mean, boy, it's dashed unreasonable to expect me to hold a conversation with you while I'm standing up and you're squatting on the road like a sniveling hedgehog! Get up so that at least I can see your face."

Hastily, Davie scrambled to his feet, Bonnie still locked securely in his arms. He was taking no chances. Warily, he darted a glance behind where the colonel stood. The shepherd dog, Juno, was crouched on the ground, her head between her front paws, her dark red eyes unwinking. She was on a leash now, the end of which was firmly held in Colonel Blaikie's right hand.

The tall man cleared his throat; then, removing a handkerchief from his pocket, blew his nose like a bugle. He frowned as though he was having difficulty getting the words he wanted to say in the proper military order. "Sorry, boy." He gave a loud *hurr-umph*, then tugged with annoyance at the end of his mustache. Quite clearly, Colonel Blaikie was not accustomed to apologizing. He glowered at Davie, thrust his left hand deep into his pocket, then shriveled his red face into a massive frown. "Where were we, boy?" he demanded testily.

Davie said carefully, "You were saying you were sorry, sir."

"Eh! I was? Well, confound it all! I mean, how was I to know Juno would get upset about your dog? First time she ever saw one of those small collies. Maybe she took it for a weasel or something! No offense, mind you. Anyway, you can let it down now. Juno won't do anything."

"No, but Bonnie might," Davie said respectfully, with a shake of the head as he held onto his dog. "They're rare fighters, are Border collies, especially the kind we breed around Wee Clachmannan. No telling what she might do to your dog if I let her loose." He gazed up at the tall man with innocent eyes.

Colonel Blaikie looked as though he was about to have some kind of fit. His cheeks got fiery red and the ends of his mustache quivered as he slowly exhaled. "What? Are you telling me you're afraid your dog might attack Juno?" He blew out his cheeks, snorted fiercely, then strode past the boy. "Crazy!" he thundered as he proceeded up the road with Juno trotting docilely behind him. "The whole confounded world's going stark crazy!" A kite's tail of deep-throated grunts, growls, and grumbles followed him as he continued on his way to Grannoch Moor.

Davie, once he was certain they were gone, bent down and placed Bonnie on the ground. He was surprised to find that his legs were trembling and that the palms of his hands were moist with sweat. Despite the brave talk he had given the colonel, he knew it had been a very close thing indeed. There had been murder in the eyes of the huge shepherd dog as she advanced on Bonnie. It was fortunate that Colonel Blaikie had been there to call her off. Suppose, though, he had not been there? Suppose Juno should come across Bonnie in the vastness of

Grannoch Moor? Davie felt a coldness shiver down his back. He would have to be careful. If anything ever happened to Bonnie—he shuttered his mind against the dark images his imagination had released. No, he would have to be careful. Never again could he let Bonnie run free on Grannoch Moor.

Kate Cameron's eyes studied her son. "You mean, Davie, that new dog of Colonel Blaikie went for Bonnie?"

The boy nodded. He knelt on the floor in front of the fireplace and let his fingers trail between the dog's ears. Bonnie lay on her stomach, her rear legs tucked under her, her front legs extended forward as a cushion for her head. Her eyes were closed and her freckled brown nose quivered slightly as she dozed.

"Aye," he said, "or was about to. Anyway, nothing happened." He could feel the warmth from the dog's body steal up his fingers as he caressed the black-and-white coat. This was the way it had always been, as long as he could remember—the two of them before the fireplace and the flames leaping like startled fireflies up the black chimney. Only always before he had felt secure and content. Tonight it was different. For a reason he could not have explained, it seemed cold in the kitchen. As

25

though a door had been suddenly opened. Only he knew the door was soundly locked against the night air. And yet the coldness was there. He felt it press against his heart, a coldness without end and without beginning.

He shook his head angrily as though to dislodge the ugly thought that clung like a burr to his mind. It was daft! So Colonel Blaikie had a new dog! So what of it? Besides, Bonnie could take care of herself. Had taken care of herself since that day eight years ago when his father had first brought her home and trained her for the sheep. No, there was nothing to worry about. Anyway, Colonel Blaikie kept pretty much to himself in Grannoch Moor. Chances were he would keep a close rein on the big dog.

Kate Cameron poured herself a cup of tea. "I gave the cow the mash. She seemed to like it. At least it stayed in her stomach." She stirred her tea and did not look over at her son.

Davie smiled. "Aye, but Fergus is the clever one for certain," he said proudly. "He knows a lot about things like that, medicines and herbs and oatmeal poultices. He told me once that his sister Annie had wanted him to be a doctor."

His mother stared at him in astonishment. "Are you daft, lad? Well you know that Fergus never learned to write, poor soul. How could he ever hope to be a doctor?"

Davie shrugged. "Och, and what's the difference? Fergus himself said that many of them can't write, either. At least not in English. That's why they have to use Latin when they send their wee notes to the chemist. Aye, Fergus is clever, all right, when it comes to the healing. I mean if he can cure a sick cow, why no' a sick man?"

Kate Cameron laughed. "I'm afraid he'd have to come up with something besides seaweed mashed with oatmeal and herring. Not all patients, Davie, are as cooperative as Maggie our cow." She took a sip of her tea. "Anyway, I'm fond of old Fergus in spite of his odd ways at times." She got up from her chair and placed the cup on the open-topped black range. After a long silence she said carefully, "By the by, Davie, weren't you telling me that Fergus had also seen Colonel Blaikie's dog?"

"Aye. Fergus has an idea that the reason the colonel got such a dog is because of the ghost Fergus claims lives in Rowan House. In fact, Fergus told me his sister Annie had even seen the ghost with her own eyes. Of course, that was a long time ago."

His mother laughed lightly. "All those old houses have ghosts. At least that's what the owners claim when they put their houses up for sale. They get a better price when the house comes with its own resident ghost. Anyway, I don't think that's the reason Colonel Blaikie got this big dog. I think it's more likely he got her to discourage burglars. After all, it's a huge place and he can't keep his eye on all of it. Which would mean that this Juno of his has the run of the house and the grounds."

Davie frowned. "So?"

"So without any fence at all, Juno can come and go pretty much as she wants to, Davie." Her face was troubled. "I think after what you just told me maybe you'd better tie Bonnie up whenever you're not out with her."

He stared aghast. "Tie her up? But Bonnie's never been tied up! She's run free on the moor since she was a pup!"

"I know, Davie, only it was different then. She's used to coming and going as she pleases, and if it pleased her to run over to Rowan House there could be trouble. Anyway, Davie, I'll leave it up to you. You're old enough now to make decisions for yourself."

He said nothing. What was there to say? Tie up Bonnie? Bad enough to tie up a dog in a big city like Glasgow. Aye, bad enough, but to do so in the Highlands with the open hills and the glen would kill the heart of any dog. No, better to take her chance with the shepherd dog than to deny her the freedom she had always known.

"I couldn't do it. No' to Bonnie." He did not say any more, afraid to trust his voice.

He felt her fingers, a familiar softness as they brushed against his hair. "It's right you are, Davie, lad. Freedom will not be a thing that can be kept at the end of a leash. For men or dogs. Now off to bed with you. There will be much for us to do in the morning with the potatoes to be lifted and the peats to be stacked for drying." She paused. "Anyway, the cow seems better, thanks to Fergus, and that at least is something. Goodnight, Davie."

"Goodnight," he said. He was on the point of getting to his feet when he suddenly felt the dog's body stiffen beneath his fingers. The ears went back in an attitude of intense concentration, and a low growl rose from deep in her throat. Davie turned his head and listened. Nothing. Nothing but the scrape of rain against the window and the wind turning like a restless sleeper in the branches of the birches outside. Nothing more than that. And yet Bonnie had plainly heard something. Something that had aroused her from her sleep.

Davie hesitated, then, rising to his feet, crossed over and opened the door. Nothing stirred in the

29

darkness that swept in a solid wave into the immensity of Grannoch Moor. Not even a star glimmered, so that the darkness of the sky and the darkness of the earth were one and without beginning and without end. He closed the door, troubled for a reason he could not explain.

Bonnie crouched low on the floor, her hair bristling, her gums drawn tightly back so that the teeth gleamed with a stark whiteness in the flickering light from the fireplace.

Her body suddenly quivered as though a wind, cold from Grannoch Moor, was passing over her.

Chapter 3

"Och, and it's very simple, Davie," Fergus said, his eyes fixed on the small whaling boat which he was carving from a piece of bleached driftwood. "As ye know, many dogs, like people, have the gift of the second sight. They can sense things that have still to happen. My sister Annie had the gift."

"She did?"

"Aye. No' that it's always a good thing, mind ye. She saw her own death three weeks to the day before she died. Only she wouldn't let on to me, her knowing how I felt about her and the loneliness that would be there when she was gone. She was aye that fond of me, was Annie." He laid down the whaling boat and brushed his hand across his face.

"No, Davie, to know the future is not always a good thing. Some things are best not known."

Davie stirred uncomfortably on the bench against the rough boards of the cabin. He did not like all this talk about death. Still there was no denying that no one in Wee Clachmannan knew as much about the supernatural as old Fergus Gow. When he had lots of cheese in him and he could think clearly, he could tell you endless stories about the little folk who dwelt under *Croc an t-Sithein*, the hill of the fairies. Yes, and about the seal people whose home was the sea just off the coast of the Hebrides. Mostly they were sad stories though, like the one about young Murdo Campbell who had been bewitched into a merman and nightly returned to the shore fronting the village he had left, crying plaintively to the lass he had loved and would never see again. Perhaps though, as Fergus said, the stories were sad because the world itself was sad. In many ways, Fergus had never really gotten over the loss of the sister who had cared for him and protected him fiercely against the world. Once he had told Davie that he often left the door of the cottage open at night, just in case Annie's spirit felt like dropping in. He always left a plate of cheese on the table, too, for Annie had loved cheese just as passionately as Fergus.

Davie, in an effort to put aside the gloomy thoughts that filled his mind, let his eyes wander aimlessly around the cabin. He stared, quite without seeing, at the rafters overhead from which hung a string of dried salt fish, a patch of herring net, and a pair of wind-bleached dungarees. Pieces of driftwood were piled high around the base of the kitchen walls and a handful of damp peats glowered sullenly from the blackened hearth. Litter and old picture magazines covered the floor and a pail behind the door overflowed with bottles, cans, and potato skins. The room was a shambles of odds and ends except for the corner that held a recessed bed. That had been where Annie slept. Nothing had been touched since that day three years ago she had taken her leave from her brother. It was the only time she had ever left him. The faded yellow bedspread had been smoothed out and the pillow was fresh and uncreased. The bedspread and the sheets had been neatly folded back, almost as though Fergus expected his sister to return at any moment. Perhaps he did.

Davie had taken his leave and was halfway up the path from the kelp-snarled beach when he heard Fergus' voice. "I would keep an eye on your dog, just the same, Davie Cameron. It will be doing no harm at all."

"I will, Fergus." He waved, and breaking into a trot, headed back home across the thick, tussocky grass with Bonnie loping at his heels.

The afternoon went by on eagle's wings for there was much to do around the croft. Maggie, the cow, was greatly improved but, like the stubborn Highland female she was, refused to eat anything but the mash as suggested by Fergus. This meant a trip to the village for more herring, and after that his mother sent him out to dig potatoes. After he had done this for two hours he placed the potatoes in pails and carried them to the shed alongside the croft. Kate Cameron had already covered the floor of the shed with dry hay, peat dust, and layers of bracken and heather. Davie placed the potatoes on the soft bed, then covered them with another layer of heather. He was conscious of a warm feeling deep within him as he regarded his efforts. It was good to know that the potatoes would be safe for the dark winter nights when the snow would cover the barren ground around Wee Clachmannan. He stopped only long enough for a glass of milk and a thick scone coated with butter. Only after he had finished his chores and shaken the dust from his shirt and trousers did he realize Bonnie was nowhere around.

He frowned. It wasn't like Bonnie to go off and

leave him. Normally, the little collie stayed by his side, content to follow him wherever he went. It was for that reason he had not bothered to tie her up, certain she would stay close to the cottage. He looked around uneasily.

"Bonnie!" he called. "Here, lass!" He waited. There was no stir. He called again. Louder this time. Again no response. He stood, undecided, conscious of a vague sense of unease deep within him as his mother came out of the cottage after cleaning the butter churn. She set it in the sun to dry. "Have you seen Bonnie?" he asked.

Kate Cameron glanced around. "Bonnie? Wasn't she with you?"

He shook his head. "Haven't seen her since I came back from Fergus' place."

"She'll come back. She's always come back," his mother said, a little too briskly. "Probably went down to the butcher's. That man fairly spoils her. It's a wonder at all that the dog can move with all the scraps of meat he keeps giving her."

"Will you be minding if I stop now? I've finished the potatoes." He hesitated, forcing his voice to a casual timbre. "I was thinking I could use a walk for myself. Maybe get some of the peat dust out of my lungs."

If she had read his thoughts she never let on. "No

doubt you'll be running across Bonnie while you're out. Don't be late. It's dulse soup tonight with herring and potatoes."

He tugged off the heavy gum boots he had been using and tossed them next to the door. He was not thinking of dulse soup and what went with it. He was thinking of Bonnie. It was odd the way she had taken off. It wasn't like her. Maybe, though, his mother was right. Maybe she had taken off for the butcher's in Wee Clachmannan. Mr. Cruikshank *did* spoil her. Davie nodded to himself. Yes, that was it. He would no doubt find her in the butcher's, sprawled on the floor and munching contentedly on a bone.

But Bonnie was not in the butcher's shop when he got there. No, Mr. Cruikshank hadn't seen her all day. Nor was she anywhere in the village itself. Davie was on his way home, perplexed and disturbed at the dog's absence, when he met Ian Chisholm, the young schoolteacher. Although Mr. Chisholm was a newcomer to Wee Clachmannan, having only recently arrived following his graduation from the university, Davie was already on excellent terms with him. Some there were in the village, though, who looked with disapproval at the young teacher with the long red hair and untidy beard. They feared he was setting a poor example

36

for the youth of Wee Clachmannan with his hippy look and his air of amused irreverence at the world around him. Davie didn't agree with this reaction. He liked the young teacher and thought he looked remarkably like the picture of his hero, Rob Roy MacGregor, the famous outlaw who had terrorized the countryside so many years ago. And come to think of it, no one had ever called *him* a hippy! At least not to his face. But then, of course, there hadn't been too many hippies around the Scottish countryside in those days.

"Will you have seen Bonnie, Mr. Chisholm?" he inquired.

"Bonnie?" The schoolmaster rested the fishing rod and creel he was carrying on the ground. "Certainly did, Davie. About an hour ago. She was all by herself out in Grannoch Moor. I was on my way back from Loch Moidart when I saw her."

"Grannoch Moor?" Davie felt his skin prickle with a quick coldness.

Ian Chisholm nodded, a bemused expression on his face. "Peculiar thing, she didn't look as though she was out for a romp. I know she saw me but she never turned her head. Kept loping straight ahead as though she was late for an appointment." His eyes suddenly lifted as he caught the look on the boy's face. "Anything wrong, Davie?"

"Eh? No. No, thank you, Mr. Chisholm. I'm sure there's nothing wrong—I'll find her."

The schoolmaster grunted. "Hope you have better luck than I had in Loch Moidart. The trout weren't biting but those blasted midges were! Most of my face feels like a chunk of raw meat. Thank goodness for my beard. At least they couldn't bite through *that*." He retrieved his rod and creel, then seemed to think of something, for his face suddenly furrowed in a dark scowl. "I can just see the sly look on Mr. MacAndrew's face when I stop in to his shop to buy some of his blasted fish! Maybe I'd better get rid of my gear first. What a day! See you later, Davie."

"Good-bye, Mr. Chisholm." Not until he was some distance away from the young teacher did Davie hasten his stride. Grannoch Moor? What could Bonnie be doing out there? And near Loch Moidart? There was nothing beyond Loch Moidart but empty moor and peat bog. Nothing, unless you counted the grim pile of stone that was Rowan House. And all at once Davie knew why his skin had gone cold a moment ago. For almost certainly the huge dog would be there—waiting. What was it Mr. Chisholm had said about Bonnie? *Kept loping straight ahead as though she was late for an appointment.*

Davie Cameron was running now. Running as he had never run in his life, indifferent to the flinty stones underfoot and the brambles that tore at his legs as he raced toward Grannoch Moor. Despite the heat of the day, he could feel the sweat, cold against his ribs, as he reached the dun-brown expanse of moor and bogland.

He was past the brooding waters of Loch Moidart now, without having seen any sign of the dog. She could not have cut back to the village since Mr. Chisholm had spotted her. That could only mean that she was somewhere ahead of him. And ahead of him now was only one thing. A huge heap of blackened rock that rose like a dark shadow from the flatness of the moor. Rowan House.

He stopped running the moment he saw the man striding toward him. Only one man around the village walked quite so erect, so purposefully. Colonel Blaikie. He was alone and he must have just seen Davie, for he suddenly veered slightly so that his path brought him directly to where the boy was standing. He paused when he came abreast of Davie.

"I am sorry, boy." He said it not ungently. "I telephoned to Dr. Menzies, the vet. He is on his way."

Davie stood motionless, his throat tight. Something had happened. He said, "It's Bonnie."

Colonel Blaikie nodded. "I'm afraid she's rather badly hurt. What on earth she was doing out by Rowan House I'll never know. Juno was loose, of course. By the time I got there it was late. Too late, I'm afraid. Your dog was fighting fiercely, not giving an inch, but Juno had a grip on her—" He stopped. "Anyway, the vet is on his way. He'll do everything he can."

"Yes," said Davie. "Yes."

Chapter 4

Bonnie died two days later. Nothing that the vet could do was enough to save her. Her throat had been too badly mauled by the big dog. When it was clear that she was beyond any human skill, Fergus had advised Davie that he would pray for her. Aye, and in the Gaelic too, for hadn't his sister Annie told him time and time again that the Lord never could get the hang of the queer English tongue? It was clear that He was much more at home with the Gaelic, no doubt because so many from Wee Clachmannan were up there with him in Heaven. Yet even Fergus' prayers in the Gaelic hadn't been enough. Perhaps, as Geordie Dalhousie, the village dike-builder and atheist observed sourly, God was no better at the Gaelic than He was at the English. Or maybe, as Fergus later confided to Davie, the Lord had simply been keeping His eye open for a clever wee sheep dog, Him being the Good Shepherd, and had merely whistled Bonnie to another pasture, fairer even than those around Wee Clachmannan. Yes, perhaps that was it.

The grief in Davie's heart in the days that followed was a living, throbbing thing. Bonnie had been a part of his world as long as he could remember. No day had ever dawned that she had not been a part of it. No day had ever ended that she had not made it more complete by just being around. And now, with a suddenness that pinched the heart, she was gone.

To Davie it seemed only fitting that Bonnie's last resting place should be in the hills overlooking Wee Clachmannan. There the two of them had gone on many a summer's day. Now they were going again, yet this time only one would return. He halted when he came to a spot in the heather and gently rested the canvas bag which shrouded the dog. Death seemed to have shrunk the body of the little collie, for it took only a few thrusts of the shovel into the harsh ground to prepare the grave. To Davie it was an odd and melancholy thing that Bonnie, who had filled so much of the world when

43

she was alive, required such a tiny part of it now that she was dead. He smoothed the small crumbs of earth over the raw wound in the heather and, rising, made his way home.

The weeks that followed passed slowly and he was grateful for the work that had to be done in the long summer days around the croft. Sometimes Fergus or Mr. Chisholm dropped around for a chat. Once even Mr. MacWheery, the dour-faced undertaker, stopped in to express his regrets at what had happened, much to Davie's surprise. Normally, Logie MacWheery spent all of his time bewailing the fact that everyone in Wee Clachmannan lived far too long and it was no place at all, at all, for an undertaker to make a decent living. Despite the stubbornness of the natives to leave the scene, Logie never moved his business elsewhere. Once he had reluctantly admitted to Mrs. Cameron that, although the pay was poor enough, the hours were not too bad. For a man who heartily disapproved of hard work, perhaps Wee Clachmannan suited Logie MacWheery a lot better than he let on.

"So Bonnie's dead," he said with a shake of his long head. He stirred the tea which Davie's mother had given him. "Och, well, and we all have to go sometime."

"That's true, Logie." Mrs. Cameron agreed.

"What I'm no' understanding at all," said the undertaker, "is why Bonnie went off by herself like that? They tell me the new schoolteacher saw her running past Loch Moidart on her way to Rowan House. Why, now, would she be doing a daft thing like that? She knew the big dog was out there waiting for her."

"Perhaps that's why she went," Kate Cameron said quietly.

"Eh?"

"Perhaps she knew something we don't. Davie here noticed her just the night before it happened. She was lying peacefully by the fire when all of a sudden she sat up, a queer light in her eyes. If it was her death she saw, it did not frighten her."

Logie MacWheery grunted, his mind on other matters. "Wish some of them around Wee Clachmannan would start having those visions! The last burial I had was when Soutar Drummond died of the mumps at eighty-eight. Aye, they keep on living just to spite me, I'm thinking." With an effort he heaved himself to his feet. "Thank ye kindly, Kate. What I just said would no' be applying to yourself. You're no' the kind that would deny a man an honest living."

She smiled. "Thanks, Logie. And thanks too for dropping over and speaking to Davie. I'm afraid he misses the dog sorely."

Logie MacWheery twisted his black bowler hat between his fingers when he reached the door. "By the by, will ye have seen anything of Colonel Blaikie lately?"

She hesitated and exchanged a quick glance with her son. "No," she said. "No."

The undertaker frowned. "The man might have called. But that's the way it is these days! Everybody's out for himself and no thought at all, at all, for anybody else. It's a wonder the Lord doesn't wipe them all out with another flood, but I suppose it would be a lot o' bother. Besides, it never really dried out from the last time. At least around Wee Clachmannan." With a doleful shake of the head and muttering under his breath, Logie MacWheery took his departure.

Until the undertaker had mentioned his name, Davie had not even thought about the colonel. His heart had been filled with too much grief, his mind too distraught. Yet now that he *did* think about it, it was strange that the man hadn't even called. Wee Clachmannan was a tight little community, and although Colonel Blaikie was a newcomer and lived remote from the village, he certainly was familiar with the local customs. He also knew how much Wee Clachmannan respected and valued its dogs.

Generations of Clachmanians had bred collies, and prized a sound dog above all else. Yet since Bonnie's death Colonel Blaikie had kept himself aloof from the villagers, as though washing his hands of the whole affair. True, he had called the vet when he had known how badly Bonnie was hurt, but that was the least he could have done. Obviously, he was not interested in dogs. Or people, for that matter. Which would explain why he had bought gloomy Rowan House in the first place.

In these circumstances, therefore, Davie was unprepared one afternoon two months later when Mrs. Cameron answered a knock at the door and admitted Colonel Blaikie. He frowned, nodded indifferently in Davie's direction, and faced Mrs. Cameron.

"Permit me to introduce myself, madam. I'm Colonel Blaikie." He paused. "Of Rowan House," he added, as though afraid she might get him somehow confused with some other Colonel Blaikie around Wee Clachmannan.

Davie's mother smiled. "Yes, I've heard of you. I'm Kate Cameron. Please come in."

He advanced two steps into the kitchen, then paused, his eyes flashing. "I want you to know, madam, I am not here to apologize! While I am sorry for what happened, your boy's dog had no business on my property. Juno has been trained to protect Rowan House. She was only doing her duty."

"A cup of tea, Colonel?" Kate Cameron did not wait for his reply but put the pot on the table, and a cup and saucer. She removed a griddle of scones that had been hanging over the peat fire. "You'll find some butter and cheese over there above the dresser. Help yourself."

Again he frowned. Clearly this was not the reception he had expected. "Nothing, thank you, madam," he said stiffly. He looked around the kitchen, plainly at a loss for words and unsure of what he wanted to say. "Look here, Mrs. Cameron, I'm a blunt man and I like to speak my mind."

The ghost of a smile touched her lips. "Blunt men usually do," she said. She stirred a cup of tea. "Sugar and milk?"

"No sugar. No milk. Nothing, madam! Now, as I was saying, I am a man who speaks his mind. I do not sneak behind words and pretend I am something other than I am. I know those idiots around Wee Clachmannan have been talking about me. Well, let them! Your dog had no business on my grounds." An indignant flush suffused his face and neck. "And I do not apologize!"

She nodded pleasantly. "Of course. Sure you

won't change your mind, Colonel? Nothing like a cup of tea, I always say." She pulled a chair over to the table. "So you came all the way from Grannoch Moor to tell us you don't apologize? Well, now, and wasn't that kind of you?" She took a sip of her beverage. "I don't think there's anything as good as a cup of strong tea when a body's upset, don't you think so, Colonel Blaikie?"

He glowered. "I didn't just come over to tell you I don't apologize! Hang it all, Mrs. Cameron, if you'd only give me a chance and stop trying to push your blasted tea down my throat, with or without sugar and milk, maybe I could explain! You see, Juno had puppies about six months ago. Before I brought her here. Ridiculous business! After all, what the devil was I going to do with a troop of sniffling, squawking pups at my heels all day? Luckily, I have a cousin in Edinburgh who breeds and sells dogs. Packed the whole blasted bunch of 'em to him!"

Kate Cameron frowned. "But I don't see, Colonel—"

"Of course you don't see!" he exploded. "You won't let me finish! Well, as I was trying to say, I felt kind of—well, sorry, about what happened. The thought occurred that my cousin might still have one of the dogs left. Not that I really expected it, mind you. Shepherd dogs go fast on the market-place. I must confess I was surprised when he told me he still had one of Juno's litter—had been unable to sell it. Seems the dog was quieter than the others. Kept to himself a lot. Dog by the name of Laddie." He made a violent face. "Oatmeal name, that! You can always change it if you want to, boy!"

Davie stared dully. "Me? Change whose name, Colonel Blaikie?"

"Confound it all, boy, your dog's name! The one I'm giving you to take the place of that little one you had. One that got herself killed." He made a rumbling noise deep in his throat and turned to Davie's mother. "Look, Mrs. Cameron, I spoke rudely to you a moment ago. About that blasted tea of yours. Some people think I have a temper, but I don't! I just happen to be right most of the time. Can I help that?"

She shook her head mildly. "Of course not, Colonel." The skin creased around her eyes as she smiled. "I mean, it's quite understandable. After all, you were a big man in the army and you've been to lots of places besides Wee Clachmannan."

He grunted and eyed her approvingly. "You're the first sensible person I've met in these parts, Mrs. Cameron! Never ran into such a collection of smug, stubborn, thick-headed idiots in all my life!" He crossed over to the door, then paused and glowered back over his shoulder. "And just because I brought this dog over doesn't mean I'm apologizing for what happened!" He breathed heavily through his nose. "I *like* giving dogs away!" He flung the door open. "Here, Laddie!"

The German shepherd must have been waiting patiently outside, for the next moment it was in the kitchen. Davie felt his eyes widen as the dog glided quietly into the room, then looked up questioningly at Colonel Blaikie. In many ways Laddie was an image of his mother, Juno. The same lean, clean-cut head and muscular neck. The same deep chest with the ribs flat and the stomach held well up. The same russet brown hair lying tight against the body. Only the almond-shaped eyes were different, and a certain expression on the face of caution and un-certainty. Davie found himself wondering if possibly the long months of rejection in Edinburgh might have had something to do with it. With the rest of Juno's litter sold, Laddie had been alone with his pride and his rejection. It might not have been easy for him, for any sensitive, highly strung animal. Davie shrugged. It was no affair of his. The dog meant nothing to him. No son of Juno, the dog that had torn Bonnie apart, could ever mean any-thing to him. Never.

"I don't have to tell you, Mrs. Cameron, that Laddie is a purebred," declared Colonel Blaikie. "You wouldn't want a finer German shepherd. Why the devil he wasn't grabbed up in Edinburgh I'll never know! Bunch of blithering idiots in Edinburgh." His heavy face mashed in a frown as he stared at the dog resting quietly at his feet. "Does seem a little remote. Not good in a dog, that! As though he didn't trust people. Well, I don't trust them either, but hang it all, Mrs. Cameron, I get along with them, don't I?"

She laughed lightly. "I'm sure you do."

He nodded. "Well, that's taken care of anyway. Your boy has a new dog. A much more expensive one than he had before." He flung open the door, then paused as some thought seemed to strike him. He frowned and darted a final angry glance at Davie's mother. "But don't think I am apologizing, Mrs. Cameron! I *never* apologize, even when I'm wrong! And I'm *never* wrong!" The door fairly quivered on its hinges as he slammed it behind him.

"Well," murmured Kate Cameron after a long silence, "and what do you think of that, now?"

Davie did not answer. His eyes were fixed on the dog resting quietly on the floor, its head cradled between its forepaws, its ears raised, its eyes watchful. Davie could feel the bitterness that seemed to gnaw

53

at his stomach with cold rat teeth. *More expensive!* As if it was a matter of money. How did one go about hanging price tags on things like love and trust and the memory of Aprils shared on wind-swept hills? And there was something else. Something that could not be forgotten. Would never be forgotten. It was the mother of this dog lying here on the kitchen floor who had killed Bonnie. Bonnie. . . .

He said tonelessly, "I'm no' wanting him. I don't want another dog now that Bonnie's gone. Besides—" He stopped and did not finish the sentence.

"I know what's on your mind. That it was Laddie's mother who killed Bonnie. But that is not fair, Davie. It was not Laddie and you cannot blame the dog for it."

"No," he said. He kept his eyes from where the dog lay. "I'm thinking though we should give him back to Colonel Blaikie. He would no' be happy here at all."

She gave him a troubled look. "But we can't do that, Davie. The colonel would be hurt and in his own way, he meant well."

He said nothing. What was there to say? His mother was right of course. It wasn't Laddie's fault. He understood that. Just as he understood that never could he hope to love this dog. Never.

"The dog stays," said Kate Cameron quietly.

54

Chapter 5

The months which followed were not happy months for Davie Cameron. Studiously he avoided the dog and had as little to do with him as possible. Yet try as he might, he could scarcely ignore the dog's presence around the house. For one thing, Laddie had grown taller and more powerful since the day that Colonel Blaikie had brought him over to the cottage. He was quick and intelligent and, once shown something, never had to be shown again. Yet, although he was still a comparatively young dog, there were none of the flashes of playfulness that one so often finds in German shepherds of that age. He lay quietly, searching Davie's face, perhaps waiting for some sign, some signal that would bridge the gap between them. When none came, the dog retreated more and more into that remoteness that the colonel had remarked on. The dog seemed to accept Davie's coolness as a fact of his world. He made no effort to follow when the boy left the cottage. Only the eyes, like dark smoldering coals, hinted at the hurt as the door closed behind the boy.

It was not that Davie was ever unkind to the dog. He could not have found it in his heart to be deliberately unkind to any dog. He fed Laddie himself and made sure that his sleeping rug was aired daily. Although he disliked doing it, he saw that the dog was groomed regularly, so that his coat fairly glistened in the sun. The ticks, nettles, and burrs that Laddie occasionally picked up were removed by Davie before they could irritate the dog. All of these things the boy did faithfully, if they were not done cheerfully. To Davie, they were simply chores that had to be done. Like peat stacking and potato lifting. Nothing more than that. Or at least, that was what he told himself. Yet why was it that, whenever he left the dog to go its own way, there was always a sense of shame deep inside him? On more than one occasion he had to force himself to remember that it was this dog's mother that had killed Bonnie. True, it hadn't been Laddie's fault. Yet there it was. To have accepted Laddie would mean that, in some way, he was rejecting Bonnie.

But although Davie could steel his heart against pity for the young dog, he could not blind his eyes to Laddie's grace and elegance. Never in all his life had he seen a dog so handsome and with such perfect lines. With puppyhood behind him, the breed lines had become more prominent. The forehead was more noticeably arched with the skull sloping and continuing into a finely pointed muzzle. The chest had grown deep, but not excessively broad, and the back was flat and in precise proportion to shoulder height. The dog carried his eighty pounds with the smooth, rhythmic gait of the true shepherd. Everything about him proclaimed his heritage. Only the almond-shaped eyes were different —the eyes that, curiously lifeless, stared at the boy every time he left the cottage without casting a glance behind him.

Although Laddie was free to come and go as he pleased, he now rarely stirred from the cottage. He seemed to have no interest in the mountains and glens that had been such a part of Bonnie's life. On rare occasions he trotted down to Wee Clachmannan but again, unlike Bonnie, he did not visit with the shopkeepers and pass the time of day with the old men on the benches by the Post Office. Why he went at all was a mystery to Davie, for he seemed to avoid the villagers and even cheerful Mr. Cruik-shank, the butcher, had given up tempting him with scraps and sweet-sueted bones. For some curious reason his visits to Wee Clachmannan always took place when Davie himself was in the village. The thought had crossed the boy's mind that it had been more than chance that had brought the dog there at these particular times. But Davie shrugged. It made no difference to him where the dog went and, whenever he chanced upon Laddie in Wee Clachmannan, he made no effort to invite the dog to go with him. Before long, Laddie gave up his visits to the village and no longer stirred from his place by the fire when the boy left the cottage.

Autumn slid into winter, and soon the wind from the north was alive with snowflakes like churning confetti. The light started to seep from the sky in the early afternoon and the nights were long and bitter cold around Wee Clachmannan. Winter was a time of silence around the moor, for the streams were mute with ice and the birds and the leaves were gone from the trees. What sounds were left were soon buried under the thick fleece of snow that covered the land. In the dark hours, time passed slowly for Davie Cameron, although there was always something to do around the cottage after school. In the long nights after supper he busied himself with whittling and helping his mother fashion the heather brooms she would later sell to the summer visitors. He accepted Laddie's presence around the house as he accepted the darkness and the leaden skies and the winds threaded with sleet and snow that blew endlessly in from the vastness of the Atlantic.

Spring came late to Grannoch Moor, catching the barren trees by surprise and splintering the ice in Loch Moidart into a field of winking diamonds. Mornings broke against the hills in long amber waves, spilling fine sprays of light across the awakening fields. Davie could feel the new softness in the air and the stirring of life all around him as the sun rose stronger in the eastern sky and the warm rains came to knead the harshness from the earth.

Yet, if spring brought new life to the countryside around Wee Clachmannan, it wrought no changes in the big shepherd dog. Laddie, if anything, seemed more spiritless and indifferent. He ate only when he had to, and left the house even less frequently than before. Many a time Davie turned suddenly to find Laddie's eyes fixed gravely upon him, but other than that, the dog seemed resigned to the life around him and no longer made any effort to follow the boy. It was Davie's mother who announced one evening in late April that Laddie was nowhere around.

"Laddie?" Davie tossed his schoolbooks on the table. "He'll be back. Maybe he just took a run for himself in the hills."

Kate Cameron shook her head. "It's not like him. He left just after you went to school. Usually he sits by the fire all day and rarely leaves the grounds." Her eyes were troubled. "Poor Laddie! I hope nothing happened to him."

He grunted. "You're daft, surely. Just think of the size of him! How could anything happen to the likes of that! He'll be home soon enough when he's hungry, never fear."

But when darkness came, Laddie had still not returned. Davie tried to make light of it, asserting the dog had just taken off now that the weather had turned and would be back in the morning.

"I hope you're right, Davie," his mother said. "Poor thing, he's never been out alone on the hills at night."

Davie shrugged. "What's going to happen to him? Anyway, I'll leave the door to the peat shed open. Just in case he comes back before we're up." He hesitated, then picked up Laddie's dish and placed a few chunks of meat into it. "Maybe he'll be hungry," he said a little too loudly. "Don't want him barking and waking everybody up."

She looked quickly at her son, then let her eyes drift away from his face. "That would be nice, Davie."

"And while I'm at it, I suppose I ought to leave him some milk and water," he continued in a grumbling voice. "Och, and a lot of fuss over nothing! Just you wait and see!" For a reason he could not have explained to himself, he picked up Laddie's rug later on when his mother wasn't looking and smoothed it out in the shed. He left the door wide open so that Laddie would have no trouble in gaining entry to the peat shed. He placed the meat, the milk, and the water alongside Laddie's rug and made his way back to the cottage.

The next morning when he got to the shed it was to find that nothing had been touched. Nor had anything been touched when Davie returned from school that afternoon. It was strange. Not only that Laddie had vanished, but that no one around Wee Clachmannan had seen anything of him since his disappearance. To Davie, that was the most baffling aspect of the whole business. How could a huge dog like Laddie disappear without *someone* seeing him? Clearly, he had not gone to the village. Which left Grannoch Moor and the surrounding hills. Yet no one had seen him there, either.

"It's odd," mused Ian Chisholm later that afternoon in his cottage. He fished into his jacket for his pipe. He smoked in silence for a few moments, his thoughtful eyes following the little coils of smoke rising above his head. "Not just where Laddie could have gone to, but why he took off the way he did. Dogs, and intelligent dogs like Laddie, don't just run off for the fun of it."

Davie felt the redness burn his cheeks. "He was well fed," he said, aware of the edge of defiance in his voice.

The young schoolmaster nodded. He said nothing.

"He had a good place to sleep."

Ian Chisholm sucked on the stem of his pipe. His eyes were half-closed as they followed the smoke tendrils climbing up to the rafters.

"And I never did anything mean to him, Mr. Chisholm. He went his way and I went mine."

"I see," said the schoolmaster finally. He was no longer looking at the smoke rings, but at the boy across the way. "So there was no reason at all why he should want to run off, eh, Davie?"

Davie shifted his feet uneasily. "Well, no, Mr. Chisholm. I mean—" He stopped, not quite sure what he did mean.

"Yes?"

Davie took a deep breath. "Och, now, Mr. Chisholm, and you will be knowing fine that Laddie could never have taken the place of Bonnie! Not that I minded the dog at all. I just left him alone."

"Ah," said the teacher. It could have meant anything. Or nothing.

"Maybe he went back to Colonel Blaikie at Rowan House."

"No, Davie, I phoned the colonel as soon as I learned Laddie was missing. That thought had occurred to me too. Actually, though, my call didn't make too much sense. After all, Laddie couldn't possibly know anything about Rowan House. Colonel Blaikie shipped him off to Edinburgh with the rest of the litter before he came here. As for the colonel, himself, the dog only really met him after Colonel Blaikie brought him back from Edinburgh. So Rowan House and what happened there would mean nothing to Laddie."

Davie noticed the careful way that Mr. Chisholm had avoided any reference to Juno. And, of course, the schoolmaster was right. Laddie *had* been too young to remember his mother. Too young—angrily, he snapped his mind shut against the thought that had almost breeched his defenses. "Wonder where he could have gone to?" he asked. "At any rate, he can't stay away too long. After all, he has to eat."

Ian Chisholm hesitated. He ran his fingers thoughtfully through his straggly red beard. "That is true, Davie Cameron, he has to eat." His eyes were troubled.

Davie darted a quick glance at the young schoolmaster. "Anything wrong, Mr. Chisholm?"

"Eh? No, nothing, Davie. I'm sure everything will be all right."

The troubled look was still in the eyes of Ian Chisholm when Davie left him.

Seven days came and went without any trace of Laddie. Sandy Cruikshank, the butcher's son and one of Davie's best friends, had joined him in the search for the dog but without success. Together they had scoured all of the possible spots in Grannoch Moor, yet nowhere had they chanced on Laddie's trail. Laddie was gone. Gone as utterly and completely as though he had been swallowed up in one of the deadly pools of sinking marshland that fringed Loch Moidart.

As the days passed without word of the missing dog, Davie's thoughts returned more than once to the expression on Ian Chisholm's face when he had left him. "*He has to eat*," the schoolteacher had said. What Mr. Chisholm had not said, and what had perhaps kindled the troubled look in his eyes,

64

was the knowledge that there was little game in Grannoch Moor—a few hares and rabbits, an occasional weasel. Hardly enough to support life in a big dog like Laddie. Furthermore, Laddie had never had to hunt for his food since the day he had been born. Killing to sustain life was something he had never learned. He would be helpless in the wild, unable to fend for himself. Yet, granted this was true, why had he not returned to the Cameron house where he knew there was food and shelter?

The question troubled Davie more than he liked to admit. For the only logical answer was that the dog preferred the harshness of life in Grannoch Moor to the life he had known since Colonel Blaikie had left him at the cottage. Davie knew that the fault was his, for his mother had gone out of the way to be kind to Laddie. He sensed, too, that Mr. Chisholm, whose friendship he valued, felt that he, Davie, had been wrong not to take the dog to his heart as he had taken Bonnie. Yet how could he? There had only been one Bonnie, his father's dog, and it was Laddie's mother who had torn her apart. How could he have affection for this powerful, smoothly muscled animal whose every look and movement reminded him vividly of Bonnie's killer? It was too much to ask, even though it had not been Laddie's fault that Bonnie was dead. He had treated the big shepherd decently enough. He had denied it nothing except love. Why was it somehow *his* fault that Laddie had run off? The more he thought about it, the more resentment he felt. And the more resentment he felt, the more acutely was he aware of his own sense of guilt and shame.

While the mystery of Laddie's disappearance continued to tantalize the villagers, it was quite clear that the dog's absence was no mystery at all to Logie MacWheery, the undertaker. "It's as plain as the pennies in a dead man's eyes," he announced to Davie three weeks later, "that your dog is no' anywhere in Grannoch Moor. He would be dead by the now, him as big as a pony and nothing to eat but a measly rabbit or two."

"But if he's not in Grannoch Moor, Mr. Mac-Wheery, where could he have gone to?" Davie asked.

"Glasgow!" the undertaker exclaimed. "These big German dogs are brainy beasties. Laddie knew there was nothing for him around Wee Clachman-nan at all. That's why the same one is up and away to the big city with the grand lights that stay on all night. Aye, Davie Cameron, I should have been half as brainy! I should have gone long ago to Glasgow myself and opened up a wee undertaker shop on Sauchiehall Street. I would have made a fortune,

66

the way people die there!" He scowled around at the row of coffins on display in his shop. "Look at these coffins! Dead inventory! I can't get my money back till they die in Wee Clachmannan and they'll just no' die. It's no fair—"

"But Mr. MacWheery," Davie interrupted, "what could Laddie do in Glasgow?"

"How do I know? What do I do in Wee Clachmannan? Nothing! Anyway, if your dog was out in Grannoch Moor, somebody should have seen him by the now." Logie MacWheery took off the black bowler he always wore, even in his shop, and polished it with his elbow. He blew some specks of imaginary dirt from the brim before returning the hat to his head. "Besides, ye will be minding what I said before, the dog has to eat. And there's little enough to eat out in Grannoch Moor and that's for certain."

"Yes," said Davie, glad at least that the conversation was back from Glasgow, "and Laddie's an awfully big dog."

But Logie MacWheery was not listening. His dark eyes were fixed moodily on the stacked, empty coffins, and his thoughts were apparently on other matters. "Maybe the Lord might be kind enough and send a plague. Like when he killed all those Egyptians in the Bible." He shook his head sorrow-

fully. "It's no fair at all, Davie Cameron, that a good Christian businessman like myself has to suffer like this. It wouldn't have to be a big plague with locusts and heathen things like that. Just a simple wee plague that would help me fill all those empty coffins. That's no' much to ask, is it, Davie?"

Davie smiled and shook his head. He liked Logie MacWheery and knew that he talked more because he enjoyed to hear his own solemn voice than to convince anyone. Maybe being an undertaker, Mr. MacWheery wasn't used to having anyone talk back to him. Still, Davie had to admit that the undertaker was right about one thing. Laddie had to eat. And if Laddie was not in Grannoch Moor, where was he? It was a question that continued to tease Davie's mind no matter how often he sought to dismiss it. It was a question that was still there a week later when the knocker sounded on the kitchen door.

"Fergus!" Davie exclaimed when he recognized the visitor. "Come away in."

Fergus looked uncomfortable. The gaze of his little eyes slid around the kitchen. "I have news of Laddie." He did not move from where he stood in the door.

It was strange. Davie should have felt nothing. He really didn't care. Yet, a trickle of something like relief was making its way along his nerves. He remained silent, afraid to test the timbre of his voice, and waited for old Fergus Gow to go on.

Fergus said, "They just found the bodies of two newborn lambs out in Grannoch Moor, Davie. Och, and they had been torn something terrible, the poor things! They belonged to Mr. Stewart, the factor, and he's in a rare temper I'm telling you."

Davie frowned. "But you said you had news of Laddie?"

Fergus wet his toothless gums. "That's the news, Davie Cameron. They're saying that it was Laddie who killed the lambs."

Chapter 6

"Laddie?" repeated Davie. Then for a reason he could not have explained, "But why Laddie? Did anybody see him?"

Fergus tugged at his nose as though carefully weighing the question. "No," he said finally. "Not that I'm knowing."

"Then why blame the killings on Laddie?"

The old man scratched his head. He looked unhappy. "Why now do you ask me all these questions, Davie Cameron? Life would be a lot easier, I'm thinking, if everybody didn't go around asking questions." His face screwed up in a frown. "As for Laddie, they've got nobody else to blame. And besides, the poor beast has to eat like you and me."

"He had to eat before, Fergus. What did he do before the April lambs were born?"

Fergus grunted. "Another question? I suppose, now, he caught rabbits and hares. There's no' too many of them, though, in Grannoch Moor, and maybe he's running out of them."

Davie nodded. It made sense. If anything made sense. And why was he defending the dog? It was nothing to him. Had never been anything to him. No doubt Mr. Stewart, the factor, was right. Despite his lack of experience in outdoor survival, Laddie had somehow been able to find enough game to keep from starving. Now, with the beginning of spring and the ewes weakened from the rigors of the long winter and the lambing, it would be a simple matter for a bold animal to strike. Especially a hungry one. Yes, it all made sense and yet—

"Sure you won't come in, Fergus? My mother should be home soon. She's putting on a dumpling. You like dumpling, Fergus?"

The old man hesitated. "No. Maybe that's because I never ate dumpling."

Davie found his eyes widening. "Never ate dumpling? But if you never ate it, how do you know you don't like it?"

Fergus winked. "Now, lad, tell me this. If I liked it, wouldn't I miss it?"

"Yes, but—"

"And I don't miss it. And that shows I wouldn't like it," Fergus concluded triumphantly. "Besides, there's another thing, Davie Cameron. If I *did* like dumpling, chances are I'd never be able to get it again. What's the sense o' taking on any more fancy tastes at my age? Fair sinful it would be. Anyway, I've got my cheese and nobody should want more in life than that." He hesitated before he drew the door shut. "As for Laddie, I'll wait and see. Once I saw an eagle killing a lamb. Aye, and I've seen the hoodie crows go after the eyes of the spent sheep themselves after the lambing. It's no' an easy life for man or beast, as my sister Annie used to say, and truer words were never spoken than that, Davie." The door made a soft *click* as he took his departure.

Davie stood quite still after the door had closed, his mind an overturned beehive of buzzing, stabbing thoughts. So Laddie was a killer, or so they claimed. Somehow it should not have surprised him and yet, strangely, it did. Furthermore, it was hardly fair to brand the dog as a killer if he had slain only to survive. On the other hand, he didn't have to kill to eat, he could always have come home. Davie felt a surge of the old feeling of shame and hot resentment deep within him. The dog had turned his

73

back on him. Harsh or cruel as life might be in Grannoch Moor, Laddie seemingly preferred it to life with Davie Cameron. The knowledge made his resentment all the more bitter. Served Laddie right if Mr. Stewart caught up with him!

But Mr. Stewart didn't catch up with him. The slain lambs were followed a week later by two others, both from the farm of Robbie Campbell. In each case, the attacker had sneaked up when the shepherd was elsewhere. By now all of Wee Clach-mannan was up in arms over the killings. Not only did the village depend on the sheep for its economic survival, but a killer on the loose might well become a leader of a dog pack. The last thing on earth that

Wee Clachmannan wanted was a pack of killer dogs, who had tasted sheep blood, stalking the flocks around the village.

With every shepherd and sheep owner now on the alert, the wily attacker halted his activities for the next few days. Apparently, he was studying the situation, sensing out the new defenses so that he might strike at their weakest points. And strike he then did. In the great reaches of Grannoch Moor and the surrounding hills, it was impossible to keep all of the sheep constantly under surveillance. Taking advantage of every contour and natural feature of the land, combining a capacity for infinite patience with the ability to strike audaciously at the precise moment, the killer slowly added to the number of his victims. Not a farm was immune as the attacker struck first at one end of Grannoch Moor and then at the other. So stealthily did he move and hide his traces, and so successful was he in concealing his presence from the shepherds and their dogs, that at no time had anyone caught the merest glimpse of him. He moved only when the wind was right for his purposes and he vanished as quickly as he came. It was hardly to be wondered at that the crafty marauder was soon known to every sheepherder around Wee Clachmannan as the "Ghost of Grannoch Moor."

It was agreed on all sides, of course, that the ghost was Laddie. It had to be, even though no one had seen Davie's big shepherd dog. But then, who ever saw a ghost? Besides, it was quite obvious that it had to be Laddie. The killings had started shortly after he had vanished into the depths of Grannoch Moor. He had to eat if he was to live, and what better way to eat than by killing ewes and newborn lambs?

Yet it soon became clear as the killings mounted that it was more than hunger that provoked the attacks. Too many carcasses were found, ravaged and brutally mauled, yet with the flesh largely untouched. Whatever his motivation in the beginning, it was all too evident now that the killer's principal purpose was to kill, and to kill savagely and ruthlessly. This was a new development and one that fanned the flames of hatred already burning in the hearts of the local sheep farmers.

By now all of Wee Clachmannan was enlisted in the battle against the stealthy killer. Day and night the armed patrols went out into the moor and the surrounding hills. Yet always they returned baffled and dejected without having even caught a glimpse of the phantom slayer. Yet despite the vigilance of the guards, the killings went on and scarcely a day passed without its victim. And always death had come silently and with a blinding suddenness that gave the sheep no chance to emit even one last desperate bleat of terror and alarm.

"It's uncanny," Ian Chisholm remarked to Davie one afternoon as he sucked on his pipe and leaned against the dry-stone dike outside his cottage. "He seems to know exactly every move we make. The sheep dogs we've taken out on the patrols are the finest in the village, the keenest and most alert we've got, yet not once have they raised the scent of this mysterious Ghost of Grannoch Moor. It's as though our phantom friend was sitting out there somewhere, reading our minds, men and dogs alike, and knowing everything we plan to do. He has killed thirty ewes and lambs already and, from the look of things, he'll kill a lot more before he's done." He tapped his pipe into his cupped hand. "If he's *ever* done."

"You don't think, Mr. Chisholm, it could be more than one dog? I'm thinking that thirty sheep are a lot for one dog to kill."

"You mean a pack, Davie? I doubt it. The more dogs involved, the likelier it would be that one of them would be spotted. Everything about these killings points to the work of one animal—an animal of high intelligence with an almost supernatural instinct for preservation. I think he was well named the Ghost of Grannoch Moor." He paused, thrust his dead pipe into his jacket pocket, then brushed the back of his hand across his red beard in a reflective gesture. "And of course it has to be Laddie, no question about that."

Davie said nothing for a long moment. For a reason he could not have explained, even to himself, he didn't want it to be Laddie. Yet if not Laddie, who? He knew in his heart it *had* to be Laddie. Only his mind, which he could control, refused to accept the evidence. He said, an edge of stubbornness to his voice, "Mr. Stewart and the others, they claimed in the beginning it was Laddie because he had to eat. Yet the sheep that are killed now aren't eaten at all. Only a little."

Ian Chisholm shrugged. "It was different in the beginning. Laddie was hungry. You'll remember it all started with the newborn lambs. Then from the lambs, emboldened, he went for the ewes. And once he had the sheep taste in his mouth, he turned into the wanton killer he now is. They say that once a dog has the lust for sheep blood in his veins he never loses it. It is an incessant urge that can only be slaked by blood and more blood."

"Laddie never killed anything," Davie said, then added, "when he was home." He didn't know why he said it. He hadn't meant to. After all, Laddie was nothing to him. Or was he? He could feel Mr. Chisholm's eyes on him. The schoolmaster was looking at him curiously.

"I thought, Davie, you never liked the dog? I remember once you told me you left him alone?"

The boy felt his cheeks go warm. "Of course, I never *liked* him, aye, and after what happened to Bonnie, although it wasn't Laddie's fault. It was just that Laddie went his way and I went mine."

"I see, Davie. And you don't think it's Laddie who's killing the sheep?"

"Och, Mr. Chisholm, and I don't know rightly what to think! I know everybody says it's Laddie, that it has to be Laddie, but I just can't believe he's a killer."

The young schoolmaster smiled. "Well, it would

seem to me, Davie, that right now you're the only one around Wee Clachmannan who doesn't think so. Even Colonel Blaikie, who was unusually slow to put the blame on Laddie, is now convinced. In fact, he's so afraid that Juno might run across Laddie in Grannoch Moor and get the blood lust too that he's built a ten-foot wire fence the length of Juno's pen. He's afraid too that if she wanders off by herself in the moor some trigger-happy idiot would mistake her for the killer and fill her with bullet holes." He suddenly grinned. "You get the likes of Logie MacWheery running around Grannoch Moor with a loaded rifle, you've got trouble! Logie's liable to shoot at anything that moves, just to reduce the surplus population."

Davie smiled but did not answer. So Colonel Blaikie had built a ten-foot fence for Juno, he reflected grimly. Too bad he didn't think to do it sooner. When Bonnie was alive. Only it had been different then. Juno's life hadn't been at stake as it was now. He scowled off into space. Odd how people like Colonel Blaikie always seemed a lot more interested in their own problems than those of other people!

"Well, now," murmured Ian Chisholm, glancing up the road. "Speak of the devil and here he is. Logie MacWheery himself! Seems to be in a hurry, too. Can't be a funeral or he'd be wearing that black bowler of his."

"Aye, and he's got his rifle, too," said Davie.

The schoolteacher nodded. "And pointed straight ahead," he remarked dryly. "If Logie keeps waving that thing around Grannoch Moor like that he's going to wind up with more corpses than he can handle."

The undertaker waved with his rifle when he saw them and Ian Chisholm's face went a trifle pale before Logie steadied the weapon. The teacher and the boy waited until Logie came abreast of them.

"I am the bearer of news," he intoned solemnly, as though reading the services over the body of a departed customer.

"You are also the bearer of a gun that's pointed right at my head," Mr. Chisholm said conversationally.

"Eh? Och, no matter, no matter, Mr. Chisholm. I'm a terrible shot, anyway. I was never over lucky wi' guns."

"Hope my luck is better than yours," Ian Chisholm said, his eyes warily regarding the rifle now slung carelessly over the undertaker's shoulder. "Wouldn't want my head to wind up as a trophy over your fireplace." He paused. "You said you had news, Logie?"

"Aye." Mr. MacWheery turned to Davie. "It's about Laddie."

Davie felt his heart skip a quick beat. "Laddie? You've seen him?"

"No, but I found this, Davie." Digging his free hand deep into his black undertaker's coat, Logie fished out a small metal square.

Davie stared at it for a long moment before understanding came. "Why, it's Laddie's dog tag! See, here's his name and his license number! Where did you get it, Mr. MacWheery?"

"In Grannoch Moor," said the undertaker, his voice and his face solemn. "It was lying in a bramble patch alongside the body of a freshly killed sheep."

Chapter 7

There was no question now but that Laddie was holed up somewhere in Grannoch Moor. No question, too, as far as Wee Clachmannan was concerned, that he was the vicious killer who had wrought such havoc among the flocks of the fine-fleeced Cheviots. Logie MacWheery's finding of the dog tag near the body of the latest victim was proof enough, if further proof had ever been needed. In the frenzy of his blood lust the dog had somehow caught his collar in the briars. The pin which secured the metal tag had been loose and had apparently slipped from the collar while he slashed at the sheep with his powerful teeth.

More bitter and determined than ever, Wee

Clachmannan threw additional men into the fight against the elusive Ghost of Grannoch Moor. In recognition of his military training and leadership abilities, Colonel Blaikie was elected to take charge of the forces allied against the killer. The colonel had protested mildly at first on the grounds that he was not a sheep owner and had no economic interest in the matter. Only when it was pointed out to him that he was by far the best man for the job, did he agree to accept. It was an argument he seemed reluctant to dispute. He lost not a moment in drawing up a system of grids that would assure that all of Grannoch Moor would be patrolled. Next, he appointed specific farmers to cover specific areas, so that there was no wastage of manpower and no terrain was overlooked in the relentless hunt for the crafty sheep killer. Finally, he made a list of all the caves and possible hiding places from one end of the moor to the other so that each would be visited and searched for any traces of the dog. It was an extremely thorough job and Colonel Blaikie had been well pleased with his initial strategy and line of attack. Quite clearly he enjoyed his appointment as Commander-in-Chief of the forces arrayed against the insidious Ghost of Grannoch Moor.

With the new security measures and the stepped-up vigilance, the sheep killer altered his tactics.

Rarely, now, did he attack by day, preferring the cover of night when he could sneak into the packed sheep pen, slash viciously at the terrified animals, then vanish in a matter of seconds into the surrounding darkness. By the time the herders could rush to the scene in answer to the piteous cries of the terrified ewes, he was gone with only the mangled bodies of the dead sheep to tell where he had been.

In answer to the new tactics, Colonel Blaikie set up nightly five posts near the pens and selected the best riflemen to man them. Meanwhile, his relentless search for the hiding place continued, without any development that would have given a clue to the sheep-killer's lair. Despite all of Colonel Blaikie's efforts, Wee Clachmannan seemed no nearer success in halting the slayings than it had ever been.

It was Andrew Maxwell, the postman, who finally came as near as anyone to finishing the career of the Grannoch ghost. Andrew was on guard one moonlit night when he spotted a gray object against the faint, smoky-blue of a thin mist. Normally, the sheep killer did not strike unless the moon was obscured, but Andrew cuddled the stock of his rifle and waited, alert for anything that might happen. Then suddenly, as he watched mesmerized, the gray object slid forward against the blue mist and slowly

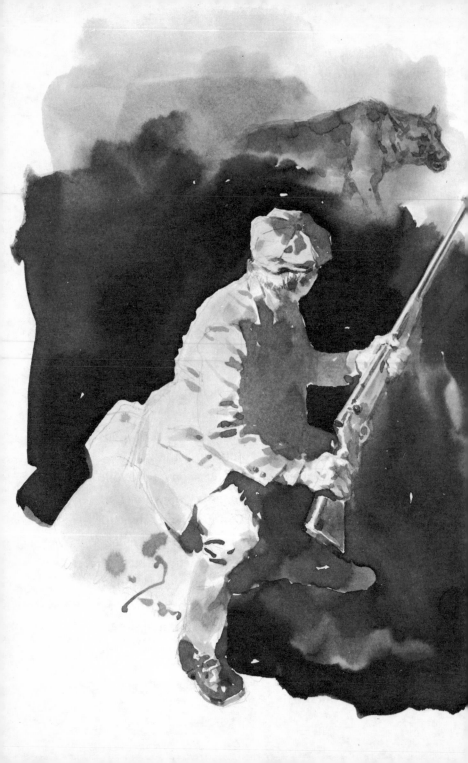

emerged into the light. Andrew froze when the creature came into view. It was a huge German shepherd dog, its powerful body slung low in a half-crouch, its legs moving stealthily and with infinite caution through a tangle of winter-sered bracken and coarse moor grass. Andrew sighted along the barrel of his rifle, took a long, deep breath, held it, and was just about to squeeze the trigger when the dog stirred. It must have sensed something, for its pointed ears went erect and its noble head lifted and half-turned in the direction of where Andrew lay concealed. The crack of the rifle and the spring of the dog were as one. Andrew let out a curse as the huge beast broke like a flash for the five-foot stone dike a few yards back in the shadows. The postman had only time for a second hasty shot before the dog was across the dike in one enormous bound and gone.

"It was Laddie, all right," Andrew had said afterward. "I'm sure of it. I may have nicked him with my first shot but I'm fearing I didn't. He was too fast altogether, I am telling you. And the way he went over that wall, och, and it was no' human at all, at all, even for a beastie! One leap and he was gone." Andrew had shaken his head, still not believing what he had just seen. "The Ghost of Grannoch Moor! He named him well who named him that, for flesh and blood couldn't have done what I saw him do."

Davie had listened spellbound to the postman's story, and had asked him to repeat it twice. So it *was* Laddie. There scarcely seemed to be any doubt about that now. Andrew Maxwell had seen him with his own eyes. Davie wondered if the postman's first bullet had landed. Andrew Maxwell was one of the best marksmen in the village. If the bullet had connected, though, it could only have been a glancing shot. There had been no traces of blood, only a few tufts of singed, wiry brown hair. Besides, if Laddie had been hit, how could he have leaped across the dike as he had?

It was queer that Davie should feel this sense of quiet relief that Laddie had escaped. After all, Laddie was nothing to him. Had been nothing to him, ever since that first day that Colonel Blaikie had brought him to the cottage. And it was all too clear he was a sheep killer, a cold-blooded monster who slaked his blood lust at the expense of harmless ewes and lambs. No crime in the Highlands was worse than that, no sin more unforgivable. Davie knew that. After all, his father had been a sheepherder. Davie also knew or sensed that somehow Laddie's guilt was mixed up with something he, himself, had done. If he had opened his heart to Laddie that first day, all of this might not have happened. Whenever he thought along these lines, he felt the fires of self-righteousness deep inside him smolder into flame. *It wasn't your fault*, he reminded himself. *You did nothing to Laddie. You left him alone.* What was wrong with that? Nothing! Yet, there it was. The feeling that, despite everything he had done or not done, somehow he and Laddie were now closer to each other than they had ever been would not leave him.

"That's right, Davie, traps." Ian Chisholm scrubbed his scraggly beard with a big red hand and frowned. "It's been a week now since Andrew Maxwell got off that shot. Since then, nothing. Nothing, that is, except two more dead sheep. So Colonel Blaikie has decided that the only way left is to set traps and hope to get Laddie that way." He pushed a plate of scones and a jar of marmalade over to the boy. "Help yourself."

"Thank you, Mr. Chisholm, but I'm no' hungry at all," said Davie. All of a sudden he had lost his appetite. Traps! He had always hated them. Cold metal things with cruel teeth that bit into the very soul of the poor trapped creature in their vise. He had seen sprung traps, where the tortured animal had escaped by gnawing through its imprisoned leg, leaving the bloody stump behind. Once he had stumbled upon a wildcat caught in a snare concealed beneath a screen of dried grass. There had been a look of such hate and pain and cold fear in the eyes of the trapped creature as had troubled him for days. And now they would set traps for Laddie. No, Davie didn't feel like eating. Now, or ever. He suddenly realized that the young schoolteacher was staring at him.

"Anything wrong, Davie?"

He shook his head. "No, Mr. Chisholm. I was just thinking they might have tried some other way of getting Laddie. Traps, they're cruel things, I'm thinking."

"All killing is cruel, Davie, I'm afraid. And Wee Clachmannan is losing its patience as fast as it has been losing its sheep. Clearly, Laddie is much too clever to be brought down by a shot. Colonel Blaikie didn't have much choice, really. But he said he had a particular obligation in the matter, as he gave you the dog in the first place."

Davie felt his cheeks burn. He didn't like the way the conversation was going. If Colonel Blaikie had an obligation in the matter, then so did he, Davie Cameron. It was queer how this sense of guilt and shame seemed to grow with every passing day. He said, "Who will set the traps, Mr. Chisholm?"

"Colonel Blaikie and several others. As a matter of fact the colonel wants me to cover the north end of the moor. There's a small spring there and it's hidden away under a rocky overledge. The colonel has a hunch Laddie goes there when he needs water. The area around the spring is covered with shale flakes and splintered rock so there wouldn't be any traces of footprints if anyone visited the spring. Weird as it might sound, Laddie seems to have an uncanny sense in these matters and maybe the colonel isn't far wrong in his hunch. Anyway, I've been asked to set a trap there tomorrow after school. Much as I personally dislike traps, Davie, something has to be done about the sheep killing. It just can't go on."

"Yes," said Davie listlessly. He understood that. If only it hadn't been a trap. Anything else but that. After a long silence he said, "The night Andrew Maxwell shot at Laddie—there was a moon in the sky. That's why Andrew saw him. But why should Laddie come out then? When there was a chance he would be seen? I'm thinking it was no' like him at all, Mr. Chisholm."

The schoolteacher shrugged. "Don't forget the lust for sheep blood is in his veins. When he saw them there, a whole pen full, I suppose it overcame his natural caution. It was the first mistake he's made. But he didn't repeat it. That's why we have to use the traps. There's no other way."

91

"Yes," said Davie. Mr. Chisholm was right. There was no other way. Not if the sheep killings were to stop. And they had to stop. He suddenly thought of something. "The traps, Mr. Chisholm. They will no' have any traps in Wee Clachmannan for a dog as big as Laddie. You'll have to send away for them. How could you set them up tomorrow if you don't have them at all?"

"Colonel Blaikie has them. Seems he's done quite a bit of wolf hunting in Northern Canada. They're double-jawed steel traps with a lightning-fast action. Laddie is a big dog and as powerful as the wolves for whom the traps were designed. Of course, we won't use any bait to lure him to the set. Laddie's too clever. If he smelled something that wasn't ordinarily there, even though he liked the scent, he would be suspicious and back off. He's amazingly cunning that way. So we'll simply set the trap, stake it firmly and hope for the best."

"Yes," said Davie. Then he said. "That's right. We can always hope for the best."

He wasn't quite sure he was agreeing with Ian Chisholm when he said it.

Chapter 8

Kate Cameron frowned. "Traps? I hate them, Davie. And I hate to think of Laddie caught in one of them. Still, I suppose it has to be done." Her mouth flattened at the corners and she shook her head. "Poor Laddie! Strange how I keep remembering him and the way he used to sit over there by the hearth, and the light from the fire in his soft wet eyes as though there was some kind of sadness deep inside him." She picked up a cup and put it on the dresser. "Perhaps there was."

"It was Colonel Blaikie's idea," said Davie, tasting the sourness in his voice. "He's the one who has the traps, too. Wolf traps." He didn't say any more. There didn't seem any point in saying any more.

His mother did not answer. She turned her face quickly from him, then picked up a peat and, breaking it over her knee, thrust it under the kettle hanging in the fireplace. She drew her hands across her apron before speaking. "One thing I am not understanding, Davie. I'm minding fine you said that Colonel Blaikie and the others searched all the caves for Laddie?"

"Aye, they did that."

"And yet they found no trace of the dog."

He moved a shoulder. "Grannoch Moor is big."

"Not too big that he can't get to the sheep pens when he's a mind to. Nobody has seen him, either, except Andrew Maxwell. He has to have *some* hiding place and it can't be too far away; yet where is it? Oh, well, there's no point at all in talking about it now. For with the traps, I'm thinking it's all over for Laddie. He was a fine dog and I'm only sorry it had to happen this way."

"Maybe they won't catch him."

"They'll catch him," she said flatly. "Clever as he is, they'll catch him."

The smoke from the smoldering peat must have caught at her eyes for she brushed the back of her hand across her face. "Poor Laddie," she said softly. "Poor Laddie."

It was impossible to sleep. For the third time that night Davie thumped his pillow and turned over in his bed. It was the week after the last of the traps had been set without any news of Laddie. Through his open window Davie could see a flighty moon as it peeped coquettishly from behind a fan of drifting clouds. Small sounds carried to his ears. The wind scurrying on quick rat-feet over the leaves in the birch tree. The solitary cry of a whaup from the distant marshes. The slapping of water against smooth stone in the nearby burn. And then he heard it. A thin, faint sound, more moan than cry, from somewhere in Grannoch Moor. He sat bold upright and listened. Had he been dreaming? He strained his ears but there was nothing. Nothing but the small familiar sounds he had heard before. Only these and the heavy beating of his heart. And then he heard it again, faint but clear. A cry, half human, half animal, full of pain and hurt. It was gone as quickly as it had come.

He was out of bed and dressed in a matter of seconds. Sleep was impossible anyway. The cry had come from somewhere deep in the moor. It could have been anything, of course. Perhaps even his imagination playing tricks. But it could have been Laddie, too. Laddie helpless in one of the wolf traps, begging for release from the pain and the fear that gripped him no less mercilessly than the steel jaws of the trap itself. And if Laddie were caught, there could be long days of suffering before death would bring relief—days of thirst and burning pain as the blood slowly leaked out of his mangled body. Davie, his mind filled with dark images, hesitated no longer. He picked up his father's old rifle and tiptoed across the kitchen in order not to awaken his mother in the next room. Gently, he slid back the bolt on the door and slipped out into the night.

It was crazy. He knew it. He had never loved the dog. In fact, he had rejected and spurned him. Yet, here he was now in the middle of the night making his way across Grannoch Moor because he feared the dog needed him! Without any shadow of doubt, Laddie was the sheep killer who had taken such a toll of the ewes and the lambs around Wee Clachmannan. He deserved no pity. Yet, granted all this was true, there was something about Laddie now that reached out to Davie despite the gulfs between them. There was no explaining it, even to himself. Somehow Laddie was in trouble and needed him and he had no choice but to go.

High above, the stars hung in the sky like a swarm of fireflies caught in a vast, black net. The moon had finally scudded from behind the clouds, and in the soft half-light Davie could make out the bulk of Rowan House and the row of stunted trees on the far side of Loch Moidart. And always to his ears, louder now and more insistent as he penetrated deeper into Grannoch Moor, came the cry he had heard before.

It was a simple matter to find his way. The pitiful cry was coming from the spot by the concealed spring where Ian Chisholm had set his trap. Davie was running now, running as he had never run, his breath a hotness in his lungs despite the chill in the night air. He breasted a slight rise in the flatness of the moor and then stopped dead in his tracks as his eyes took in the scene on the other side of the brae. There, in a small clearing of jagged slate and stone, crouched a huge German shepherd dog, its eyes blazing with fear and pain, its right front leg imprisoned in a steel vise. It must have heard Davie's noisy approach through the dried bracken fronds, for its head was lifted and turned toward him. Davie had to take only one look at the trapped dog. "Laddie!" he cried.

It was Laddie all right. Only scarcely the Laddie he had last seen. The dog had lost a great deal of weight and his ribs formed a noticeable arch against his shrunken stomach. Loose folds of mottled hair sagged from his neck, once so strong and muscular, and his chest was hollow and flat above his forelegs. Only the noble head was the same, the noble head from which burned the eyes bright with pain and hurt.

Laddie had recognized him in the brilliant moonlight. Davie was sure of it. The dog made no cry now. He rose from his crouch and his neck arched and his proud head lifted. He seemed to be letting Davie know that he expected no pity from him. That he asked none.

The boy walked slowly toward the dog, the rifle slung across his arm. He could see the blood now where the trap bit into Laddie's leg. He could see, too, the heavy extension chain from the trap, the extension chain that Laddie had uncovered in his desperate efforts to free himself. He paused when he was about ten feet from the dog and slipped a bullet into the rifle.

This was why he had come. To spare Laddie pain. For it was either a bullet now or a bullet later. Only between now and then would be long hours of agony for the dog. There was no escape from the fierce teeth of the wolf trap. Kinder to kill the dog now. Odd, though, he had taken so long to offer a kindness. . . .

Davie took a deep breath. He could feel the sweat from his finger cold against the trigger. He

98

lifted his head to sight the target. He had not wanted to but he had no choice if he were to kill the dog. His head raised, he found himself looking squarely into Laddie's eyes, and there was no fear there any more, only a loneliness more vast than the loneliness of Grannoch Moor itself.

How long he stood, his finger crooked against the trigger, he would never know. Finally, his shoulders slumped, and with a half-sob he slid forward onto his knees. It was no use. He could not shoot Laddie. Even to spare him pain. Even though he was the most hated sheep killer in all the long history of Grannoch Moor. Even though he had never loved him.

He put his rifle down; then, after a long moment, rose to his feet and advanced slowly toward the dog. He knew what he was about to do made no sense at all. It wouldn't solve any problems either, for if he didn't shoot Laddie then someone else would. Well, let them! Sheep killer or no, Laddie was still *his* dog, despite everything that had happened. And Laddie needed him now.

It was strange how he felt no fear at all as he knelt down beside the dog and put out his hand to the wounded animal. A dog in pain and terror can be dangerous, even toward someone who has shown it love and affection. And Davie knew he had shown neither.

"Easy, Laddie," he murmured, his voice a half-croon as he stroked the shrunken body of the dog, "easy, old boy. You know fine I would no' hurt you. I never meant to hurt you before, either. It's sorry I am about that, Laddie, och, sorrier than I can ever tell you. Now let me see your leg. There, that did no' hurt, did it? Now just stand still for a wee bit and mind no' to move at all and I'll untrip the spring here. Ah, there, it's open, Laddie! You can move your leg now, only don't try to run away. You can't go far on it and they'd follow the blood stains and shoot you, anyway. So mind you just stand there, Laddie, and I'll get you some cold water from the spring over there."

He was back in a moment, his fingers cupped and brimming with ice-cold water. Laddie supped greedily, and twice Davie went back for more before turning his attention to the damaged foot. The bone didn't seem to be broken, but it was hard to tell as the flesh around the wound was horribly torn and the hair matted with blood. He retraced his steps to the spring and dipped his handkerchief into the water. He did not bother now to admonish the dog to stay. Davie knew he would not move from the spot where he had left him.

Laddie made no movement as Davie tenderly

bathed the wound, nor did any whimper of pain break from him. Motionless, the dog crouched on the rough stones, his head lifted to the boy, an expression of what might have been wonder in his eyes.

Davie worked quietly, his mind seething and bubbling like a boiling caldron as his fingers worked over the dog. The whole thing was crazy! No sooner would he have finished stemming the blood and cleaning the wound than Colonel Blaikie and his men would be there to kill the dog. If he hadn't been such a coward he would have done the killing himself. Now, by acting as he had, he had given Laddie hope. And there was no hope for Laddie. Had never been any hope.

"There," he said finally, "it's no' much at all, at all, but it's the best I can do, Laddie." He stared for a long moment into the dog's eyes, then cradled Laddie's graceful head between his hands and slumped forward. "Och, Laddie, Laddie!" he cried, his voice almost a wail. "If only you hadn't killed the sheep at all! What are we going to do now? If I let you go, they'll kill you, for you can't run as you are, you with three good legs only. And I can't take you home with me to Wee Clachmannan." He leaned his face against the dog's muzzle. It was the first time he had ever done so.

There were tears in his eyes and it was hard for him to say whether they were his or Laddie's, so close did he cling to the dog. Then all at once he felt the dog stiffen beneath the pressure of his fingers, and a growl broke from deep in the shepherd's throat. Puzzled, Davie twisted his head to see what had excited the dog. For a moment there was nothing, only the empty sweep of moorland in the moonlight and the grotesque shadows cast by the recumbent boulders. And then he saw it. A dark, sinister figure creeping on all fours toward where they crouched. It moved with infinite slowness, the enormous head thrust forward, the teeth bared, the tail twitching evilly as it continued its stealthy advance. Only when the creature came out from under the half-shadow of the rock ledge above the spring and into the brilliance of the moonlight did recognition come. Davie felt his heart thump savagely against his ribs.

"Juno!" he cried as the great dog gathered itself together and leaped. "Juno!"

Chapter 9

For some insane reason Davie must have thrust his body between Laddie and the attacker, for the next moment he found himself smashed backward under the weight of Colonel Blaikie's powerful dog. His heel caught in the slaty soil and his leg went out and sent his rifle spinning into the rubble beneath the rock shelf. He hit the ground hard and felt a quick stab of pain sear his right knee. He groped for the rifle, then, realizing the hopelessness of finding it in the heaped up shale and thick shadow, struggled to his feet and turned to where the two big shepherd dogs faced each other, mother and son.

Like performers in an evil ballet they circled each other in a macabre dance of death. Their lips were drawn back so that the white fangs showed, and their eyes were unwinking in the cold moonlight. After her initial bold lunge, Juno was biding her time, content to wait until the right moment to slash her enemy to ribbons.

A groan broke from Davie's lips as he watched the unequal struggle. Laddie had no chance. Not only was he crippled and weakened from loss of blood but his body was spent from hunger and the rigors of life in the wild. Yet, despite the heavy odds against him, he showed no sign of fear or made any effort to flee. Here, true to his breed and his heritage, he would stand and die.

Suddenly, with a speed that took Davie's breath away, Juno struck. Her strong teeth bit deeply into Laddie's throat, just missing the jugular at which they were aimed. Only a desperate last second twist of his body saved Laddie. He tore himself loose from the fierce jaws of the other, slashing and ripping at the flanks of the big dog as he scrambled from under Juno's body.

She did not give him a moment's respite. Whirling, she threw herself with bared fangs at her son, and again Laddie's throat was ripped cruelly so that the blood trickled in crimson rivulets down his chest. Her success, though, was not gained without its price. Laddie pivoted and buried his teeth near

105

the nape of Juno's neck, barely missing the spinal cord. It took all her strength to fight herself free from Laddie's tenacious grip.

There was a new respect in Juno's eyes now as she warily circled her opponent, as if she realized that this was a dog to be reckoned with. No mongrel to be chevied like a frightened rabbit. A dog to be handled with caution. But no memory seemed to stir within her. She leaped.

Her sudden lunge caught Laddie off guard, or perhaps his damaged foot had crumpled under him, but the next moment, as Davie watched in despair and alarm, Laddie was on his back with Juno ripping and slashing at his head. With an angry snarl, the younger dog clawed and snapped his way from under the other, but his body was a mass of fearful wounds when he finally fought free. Then, without a moment's hesitation, he turned and, like a whirling dervish of savage teeth and flaying claws, hurled himself on the enemy.

In the wan light of the moon that spilled over the bleakness of Grannoch Moor, the eerie struggle between mother and son continued. Back and forth the fight swirled and eddied, with first one dog on top and then the other. Yet, gallantly as Laddie fought, it was all too clear he could not hope to win. The odds were too heavily against him. His eyes blinded by his own blood, his body ripped and torn, staggering on three legs, all that kept him going was instinct. Instinct and the blood of the breed.

Laddie was down again. Ten times he had been down before. Ten times he had been successful in breaking Juno's grip and regaining his feet. Only this time it was different. Struggle as he might, he could not fight his way clear from Juno's deadly embrace. There was death in the younger dog's eyes as he stared up at his foe, death and blood, but not fear.

Davie suddenly stiffened. His rifle! His breath a half-sob in his lungs, he threshed wildly around him amid the rock rubble. He groaned. It was useless. In the shadows and tricky light, he would never find it. Never! He glanced up and he could see the froth in Juno's white fangs as she prepared to lunge down on her defenseless foe. Davie waited, his blood cold as ice, for the big dog to drive for the throat and end the struggle. And then as he watched, mesmerized, he saw Juno stare down at Laddie and do a strange and puzzling thing. Her forepaw went out in an awkward gesture and she . touched, almost gently, the torn body of her son. The forepaw still rested on Laddie when Davie heard the unmistakable *click* of a bullet being

107

slipped into a rifle chamber. The sound had come from somewhere behind him, and Davie whirled around to face the man emerging from the shadows. It was Colonel Blaikie.

"Sheep killer!" said the colonel softly, as he raised his rifle. "Led us a pretty chase, didn't you? Well, it's all over now."

"No! Don't shoot him!" The cry broke from Davie's lips at the same second the crack of the rifle blasted his ears. Then his eyes closed and his shoulders hunched and he slid forward on his knees, his body wracked with dry sobs.

Chapter 10

"There, boy," said the gruff voice from somewhere above him, "no sense in taking it so hard. Dog had to die. She had the blood lust in her veins. There was no other way."

She? He blinked his eyes open. No, it was impossible. It just couldn't be. But it *had* to be, for there was Laddie, his chest still moving gently, still alive. And there was Juno sprawled dead on the ground alongside him, her forepaw still incongruously resting protectively on her son.

"She?" His voice was a whisper. "It was Juno?"

Colonel Blaikie grunted. "Tell you about it later. First let's attend to that dog of yours." He glowered at the boy. "He's still your dog, isn't he?"

Davie nodded. There was a tremendous peace in his heart and he didn't quite know how to say the words. "I'm thinking he's always been my dog," he said finally, "only I never knew it before." Then he leaned over and rested his face against the warmth from Laddie's body.

Colonel Blaikie pushed the ends of his sweeping mustache upward and smiled. Or at least Davie thought he smiled. It was hard to tell when Colonel Blaikie smiled, for all the lines in his deeply trenched face ran the wrong way and the fierce look never seemed to leave his light blue eyes.

"Thank you, madam. I will have another cup of tea. Hate the confounded stuff as a rule. Especially the way they make it nowadays. Blasted little laundry bags floating around in lukewarm dishwater. Bilge! That's what it is. Bilge!" He took a long sip and smacked his lips with satisfaction. "You make a good cup of tea, Mrs. Cameron," he conceded grudgingly.

"Thanks, Colonel." She smiled with her eyes. "You're easily pleased."

"Eh? I am?" He frowned. "Some people don't think so, but they're idiots, anyway!"

Mrs. Cameron replaced the tartan tea cozy over the pot. "You were telling Davie and me about Juno."

110

"Juno!" He looked down thoughtfully at his tea and all the bluster and fire were gone from his voice. "I—I never dreamed it was Juno. Everything pointed to Laddie here. His running wild in Grannoch Moor. The tag found in the briars near the dead sheep. He must have been attracted by the scent. After all, Juno was interested only in slaking her blood lust. Whether Laddie ate the flesh I don't know. I doubt it as he seemed half starved when we brought him here, and there were an awful lot of dead sheep he could have feasted on if he had wanted to."

"But what about Andrew Maxwell?" Mrs. Cameron inquired. "He claimed he actually saw Laddie."

"He was *looking* for Laddie, like everybody else in Wee Clachmannan. In the moonlight he saw a dog, a German shepherd dog. It was only natural that he thought it was Laddie. They have the same markings, too. Maxwell never gave a thought to Juno. Why should he? As far as he was concerned, Juno was safely locked up behind a ten-foot fence."

Davie looked up curiously from the floor where he lay alongside a dozing Laddie. "But how did she get out, then?"

Colonel Blaikie snorted. "Jumped! Absolutely crazy, I know, and I would never have believed it if I hadn't seen it with my own eyes last night. I don't know what woke me up. Maybe it was the same sound that woke Davie up, Laddie caught in the trap. Anyway, I got out of bed and couldn't believe my blasted eyes when I saw Juno crouched low in her pen. She seemed to be gathering herself together, then she ran the length of the pen and made a flying leap up the fence. I never saw a dog leap so high but she would never have made it if she hadn't found a spot where the mesh joined at a right angle and gave her some purchase. Once she got her driving hind legs above the support she simply scrambled the rest of the way. She must have found a similar hold on the other side to get back into the pen the other nights." He shook his head. "An amazing dog. I think sometimes she could almost read my mind. She had only one flaw, a fatal one. The blood lust that was in her veins."

Kate Cameron stirred her tea. "So you followed her last night after she left Rowan House, Colonel?"

He nodded. "Saw her kill a stray sheep. Got there too late. It was already slashed to ribbons. I knew then if I had never known before that the Ghost of Grannoch Moor was my own Juno."

It was odd. Colonel Blaikie of the fierce eyes and the harsh mouth and the loud voice didn't seem to be the type who would ever weep. Not that he was weeping now, but his head was bowed and his shoulders shook and there was a look of such misery on his face as Davie had never seen. Clearly, Colonel Blaikie had loved his dog. It could not have been an easy thing for him to have destroyed it.

"Try a scone, Colonel," invited Davie's mother, "and there's some bramble jam I just made." She paused. "What I still don't understand at all is where Laddie lived out in Grannoch Moor. Nobody ever found his hiding place."

"For a good reason. It wasn't there." Colonel Blaikie lathered his scone with jam and took a hearty bite. "What's the name of that queer old hermit fellow? One who goes around all day eating cheese?"

Davie exchanged a startled glance with his mother. "Fergus? Fergus Gow?"

"That's the one! After he learned about Juno he admitted he'd been leaving the door of his cabin open at night, and just *maybe* Laddie had spent his nights there. Old Fergus claims he left the door open to let some sister of his in. Weird! I mean, I understand this sister has been dead for years. He even went to the trouble of leaving a plate of cheese out for her at night and usually it was gone in the morning." He scowled. "Now don't tell me that dead sister of his ate it! Confound it all, who in his blasted right mind is going to come back from the dead for a plate of cheese?" He stopped suddenly and his fierce blue eyes twinkled. "Now your scones and bramble jam, Mrs. Cameron, that's different! That's worth coming back for!"

Her glance touched him lightly, almost casually. "Then why don't you?" she inquired quietly.

"Don't I what?"

"Come back again?"

"Splendid idea!" he boomed as he thumped his leg with a big fist. The cup of tea on his lap went flying off but he didn't seem to notice. "Confound it all, but do you know something? I like you, Kate Cameron! And your son Davie, a grand boy! And your scones and bramble jam! And your tea . . . Tea?" He stared down in confusion at the broken cup and saucer and the widening stain on the rug. He let out a soft sigh. "Never did learn the knack of balancing those confounded cups on my lap!"

Davie smiled. It was odd how less fearsome Colonel Blaikie was now that he knew him better. Maybe that was the way life was, though. It was so easy to misjudge people—and dogs. Of course, there would always be a place in his heart for Bonnie. Never would he forget the little collie. But that didn't mean his heart couldn't hold Laddie, too. After all, a dog doesn't ask for much space in a boy's heart. Only enough to be loved. Only enough to love in return.

He leaned over and ran his fingers gently down Laddie's bruised body. The wounds were healing, even the one that had been the cruelest and that had been there the longest. The wound he had himself inflicted.

"I'm sorry, Laddie," he said softly. "Och, and I'm *very* sorry!"

Laddie raised his head. Slowly, almost shyly, he pressed his wet muzzle into the boy's hand. Then, with a small sigh of what might have been contentment, he closed his eyes and went back to sleep.

About the Author

William MacKellar, who was born in Glasgow, Scotland, came to the United States at the age of eleven. He was educated in New York area schools and lived for many years on Long Island.

During World War II, he served for four years in the Signal Corps, three of them in North Africa, France, and Italy. A furlough in Scotland gave him the chance to revisit childhood scenes and to reawaken his interest in the Scottish countryside, which has since served as background for many stories.

In addition to his Scottish stories, he has written dog, sports, and mystery stories, as well as short stories and light verse. Some of his more popular titles are *Wee Joseph*, *A Very Small Miracle*, and *A Ghost Around the House*.

The author now lives in West Hartford, Connecticut, with his wife, two sons, a daughter, and a perky West Highland terrier named Bonnie.

About the Artist

Ted Lewin was born in Buffalo, New York, and studied art at Pratt Institute, in Brooklyn. He supported himself while in school by wrestling professionally, and, upon graduation, he was the recipient of the Dean's Medal. Mr. Lewin is married, and he and his wife, who is an artist, too, live in Brooklyn.